Da
Bi
Hall

Karen King

Scripture Union
130 City Road, London EC1V 2NJ.

By the same author
Topsy Turvy World – a Tiger Book

First published 1993

ISBN 0 86201 845 5

British Library Cataloguing-in-Publication Data.
A catalogue record for this book is available from the British Library.

Phototypeset by Intype, London
Printed and bound in Great Britain by Cox and Wyman Ltd, Reading

Make your own adventure

This book lets you be the writer. You can decide what happens to Charlie and Alan when they visit Birbeck Hall. You will be asked to make a choice at various stages throughout this book. After you have made a choice, follow the instructions to see what page to turn to next. Your choices will decide what happens to Charlie and Alan. You will be responsible for the adventures they will have. Will they win the prize for the project, get captured by the thieves, or rescue Lord Duncan and save the treasures of Birbeck Hall? It's up to you. So think carefully before you decide.

But don't worry if you make a wrong choice. The really exciting thing about this book is that there is not just one adventure, but eighteen of them. So you can always turn back and try again. Each choice leads you into a completely different adventure.

Have fun!

'Look, if we want to win the prize we've got to put in a bit of effort!' Charlie said firmly. 'And Birbeck Hall is one of the finest stately homes in England. Well, that's what Dad said anyway.'

Charlie's father, a freelance photographer, had visited Birbeck Hall the previous week, to take some photographs for a magazine assignment. Knowing that Charlie and Alan were working together on a school project on England's heritage, he had managed to get them both two complimentary tickets to visit the Hall unaccompanied. As the project had to be handed in when they went back to school on Monday, and Mr Cooper, their form teacher, had promised a prize for the best project, Charlie was eager to go. Alan, however, wasn't too keen. He could think of much better ways of spending the last couple of days of his precious half-term holidays, but he knew Charlie was right and they would have to go.

'OK,' he agreed reluctantly. 'But we don't have to spend the whole day there, do we?'

'I think we'd better,' Charlie said firmly. 'We need time to have a good look around, make some notes and take plenty of photographs. I know we've been to the library and written up some notes about a few stately homes, but it will really impress Mr Cooper if we actually visit one and stick our own photographs in the project.'

Turn to next page.

'I guess I'd better go and get ready then,' Alan said resignedly. 'I've got some film left in my camera but it hasn't got a flash so I can only take photos outside. How about you?'

'My camera's broke, but I reckon Nan'll let me borrow hers if I promise to look after it, and that's got a flash. I'll ask her anyway. Call for me when you're ready, OK?'

'OK.'

'And don't forget to bring some sandwiches for lunch!' Charlie called as Alan started walking down the path of his house. He lived next door, which was one of the reasons that they decided to do the project together. Another reason was that they got on quite well together, most of the time.

Alan raised his arm to show he'd heard her, then opened his back door and hurried inside to get his things.

Nan agreed to loan Charlie her camera. 'There's almost a complete film left, you can finish it off if you want,' she said. 'But mind you look after it, cameras cost a lot of money, you know.'

'Thanks Nan. I will,' Charlie promised. She put the camera in her backpack, along with her notebook and pen then opened the food cupboard and rummaged inside. 'Haven't we got any crisps or chocolate biscuits left?'

'What, after the way you've been eating them all week?' Nan reminded her. 'There'll be no more until I go shopping tomorrow.'

Turn to next page.

Ah well, she'd just have to make herself a cheese sandwich and buy some crisps when she was out, Charlie thought. Dad had given her five pounds last night for a guide book and souvenir, so she could buy something out of that from the corner shop.

'And mind you behave yourself, there's lots of valuable things in that place,' Nan warned her. 'Your dad had to pull a few strings to get permission for you both to go on your own so we don't want you letting him down, do we?'

'Don't worry, Nan, we won't,' Charlie promised her. Honestly, what did Nan think they were going to do? Slide down the banisters or draw moustaches on all the paintings? Anyone would think she and Alan were a couple of five year olds!

She had just finished making herself a sandwich when Alan knocked on the door. 'Ready?' he asked. 'We'd better get a move on. Mum said we've got to be back by four.'

'Quite right too, it's getting dark by then,' Nan agreed, handing Charlie her waterproof mac. 'Take this in case it rains. And mind you're careful of those roads!'

'We will, Nan!' Charlie promised, thrusting the mac in her backpack. Honestly, grown-ups did fuss! 'Come on, let's get out of here before we're given the full works,' she whispered, knowing that any minute now Nan would start on her don't-talk-to-strangers lecture.

'My mum's just the same,' grinned Alan. ''Bye Mrs Baxter!' he called as they walked out of the back door.

Turn to next page.

Both children had decided to go on their bikes as it was only a short ride and they had both passed their cycling proficiency tests at school.

'I'll have to pop to the corner shop first,' Charlie said as she wheeled her bike out of the garden. 'We've eaten all the crisps and chocolate biscuits so I've only got cheese sandwiches.'

'Same here. All I could find was fish paste and a bag of plain crisps,' Alan told her. 'So I'll have to buy something too. But why don't we wait until we get there? There's sure to be a shop selling chocolate and stuff.'

If you think they should go to the corner shop, turn to page 25.

If you think they should go straight to Birbeck Hall, turn to page 12.

It was very tempting. After all no one knew that they had found the notes and it was time Boffy and Jimbo were taken down a peg or two. Charlie could just imagine the look of astonishment on Boffy and Jimbo's faces if she and Alan won the prize. It would serve them right after bragging so much. Anyway, it wasn't really cheating was it? – Boffy and Jimbo had got all the information for their project from books and things, so why shouldn't she and Alan use it?

'That's a brill idea!' she grinned, putting the folder back in the carrier bag. 'I can't wait to see their faces when we win!'

Even Alan had to admit, as they cycled home later that afternoon, that it had been a very interesting day. They had lots of information for their project – and if they used some of the notes from Boffy and Jimbo's project they'd have a real winner on their hands.

Later that evening, Boffy and Jimbo came around to see Charlie. They both looked really upset.

'We left our project folder in the picnic area at Birbeck Hall this afternoon,' Boffy told her. 'It had all our notes and photos in. You didn't see it, did you? It was in a green carrier bag.'

If you think Charlie should own up to finding the folder, turn to page 31.

If you think she shouldn't give it to them, turn to page 79.

'But you promised you'd win a prize for me!' Sita protested. 'It's *my* lion!'

'Hush, Sita! Don't be so rude!' scolded Rashida. 'Charlie won it, so of course she must keep it!'

'But she said . . . '

'I only told you that if *you* won a prize you could keep it, Sita,' Charlie said. 'Don't you remember?'

Sita's face crumpled. 'But you promised. You know you did!'

'Sita! That's enough, or I'll take you straight home!' Rashida scolded.

Sita looked at Charlie reproachfully. Charlie looked away. It wasn't her fault the little kid misunderstood, she should have known that Charlie only meant if *she* won a prize she could keep it, not that she could keep Charlie's prize. But you did mean that, a little voice reminded her, and you would have given her your prize if you hadn't won the *lion*. Charlie pushed the thought away. Sita would soon forget once they started going on the rides again.

'Come on, let's go on the dodgems!' she shouted, running over to the dodgem car ride. 'We'll go in one car, Alan, and Rashida and Sita can go in another.'

'Your friends don't look like they feel like going on any rides,' Alan said when he caught her up.

Turn to next page.

Charlie turned back to see Rashida and Sita following them slowly. She knew that they were both really upset about the lion; Sita, because she knew Charlie had broken her promise and Rashida, because her little sister was upset. She felt a pang of guilt. But how could she give the lion to Sita now? That would be admitting to everyone that she'd lied and tried to cheat her out of the prize. Then what would they all think of her?

If you think Charlie should give Sita the lion and say sorry, turn to page 55.
If you think she should ignore the others, save face and keep the lion, turn to page 23.

Charlie agreed, so they both jumped on their bikes and set off. Neither of them had visited Birbeck Hall before, but Alan had been to Wykingham several times, and from there the way to the stately home was clearly signposted so they had no trouble finding it.

When they reached the ticket office, Charlie fished out of her pocket the complimentary tickets Dad had given them and handed them to the man.

'We've been expecting you two,' he smiled, ticking their names off a list, then tearing the tickets in half and handing them two halves back. 'I hope you both enjoy your visit.'

'Thanks. I'm sure we will,' Charlie said politely.

Alan noticed a pile of guide books on the counter, priced at one pound each. 'We'd better take one of those guide books, hadn't we?'

'We only need one so we'll go half each.' Charlie passed him a fifty pence coin.

The man had already taken a book off the pile and passed it to Alan in exchange for a pound coin. Then he took a cream piece of paper off another pile. 'The map comes free,' he said, handing it to Alan.

'Is there anywhere we can leave our bikes?' Charlie looked around for a rail.

Turn to next page.

'I'd cycle up to the Hall, if I were you. It's quite a way,' the man told them. 'You'll find a rail to lock your bikes onto near the main entrance.'

The children thanked him and set off down a long, winding road through parkland. At last they came to the Hall itself.

'Wow! Fancy living in a place like that!' Alan stared admiringly at the big, rambling house in front of them. 'It's bigger than all the houses in our block put together!'

'Good old Dad! We'll get lots of info for our project here!' Charlie grinned, getting off her bike and locking it to the rail. 'Come on, let's have a look inside!'

Alan was busy studying the map the guide had given them. 'Hey, there's a maze here,' he said excitedly. 'I've always wanted to go in a maze. And a waterfall. And a railway that takes you all around the grounds!' He looked eagerly up at Charlie. 'Let's have a look around the grounds first. We can see the Hall later.'

If you think they should look around the grounds first, turn to page 40.
If you think they should look around the Hall first, turn to page 18.

Charlie could see that Alan was really anxious to visit the maze so she nodded in agreement. After all, there was plenty of time to see the animals, and he was right, they probably had more chance of seeing the deer if they went a bit later.

They both studied the map and set off in the direction of the maze.

'Hey, look who's over there!'

Alan pointed to the picnic area just in front of the maze where a few families were sitting to eat their lunch. Charlie saw right away who he was pointing to. She would recognise that ginger mop of hair anywhere.

'Boffy Brookes!' she groaned. 'I bet Jimbo is somewhere around too and they've come here to get some information for the project!'

She was right. Jimbo was making his way over to the picnic table, holding an ice cream cone in each hand. He grinned when he saw Charlie and Alan. 'So you two are doing something about this place for the project too, are you?' he asked through a mouthful of ice-cream. 'Well, you're wasting your time. Me and Boffy'll win it for sure! You want to see all the notes and photos we've got about stately homes.'

They probably had too, Charlie and Alan thought crossly, glaring at their rival. Brian Brookes wasn't called Boffy for nothing. He was the class swot and always walked off with prizes for the projects. As Boffy had been away the last week of term they had both hoped he wouldn't know about the project, but they should have guessed Jimbo would go around and tell him. Those two creeps always did things together and Jimbo knew he'd win with Boffy's help.

Turn to next page.

Boffy had got up from the table and was coming over to them.

'What are you doing here?' he asked, grabbing his ice cream off Jimbo before it could melt away.

'Same as you,' Charlie told him.

'This is the third stately home we've been to this week,' Boffy said importantly. 'My mum's got a week off work so she's taken us. She loves looking around old places. She's got lots of photos and stuff she's let us use for the project.' He took a big lick of his ice-cream. 'Who did you two come with?'

'No one. We came on our own,' Alan grinned with pride at the astonished look on their faces.

'Go on, you're lying!' retorted Jimbo. 'Me mum phoned and they said no children under sixteen allowed without a grown-up.'

'My dad was working here last week and he got us special tickets to get in on our own,' Charlie informed them smugly.

Boffy and Jimbo tried not to look too impressed with this piece of news. 'Well, you're wasting your time, anyway. We've got a folder full of stuff, we'll win the prize for sure,' Boffy said haughtily, then both boys marched off to join their mothers at the picnic table.

Turn to page 20.

Charlie shook her head quickly. 'Don't be a wally! We don't need it that bad that you have to steal it!' she hissed.

Alan looked shamefaced. He knew it was wrong to steal but for a moment all he had thought of was getting the booklet, no matter what. 'I was only joking!' he bluffed. 'Crikey, you didn't think I was serious, did you?'

''Course not!' Charlie knew he had been but didn't want to make him feel awkward. She selected five post-cards showing different rooms in the Hall. 'These five cards will do. At least it will show old Cooper that we made an effort,' she said.

The lady at the till smiled at them as they handed her the postcards. 'Are you sending them to someone or are they for your scrapbook?' she asked pleasantly.

'Neither, they're for our project,' Charlie told her. 'We're doing it about stately homes.'

'Yeah, we wanted the booklet with all the photos in but we've spent all our money,' added Alan.

'On those souvenirs?' the woman smiled, indicating the paper bags they were both clutching. 'Well, never mind, I think I can help you out.' She opened a drawer in the table and took out a booklet of photos. 'It's a bit torn,' she said, holding it up to show them where some of the photos were almost torn off. 'But only along the joins, and I suppose you'd be cutting the photos out to stick in your project, won't you?'

Turn to next page.

Charlie and Alan looked at each other and then at the woman. It was just what they needed, but they only had eighty pence, would that be enough?

Alan plucked up the courage to ask. 'That would be brill, but we've only got eighty pence.'

'That's OK, you can have it for nothing,' the woman smiled and put the booklet in a bag. 'After all, I can't sell it in this condition, can I?'

Both children beamed with delight.

'Thank you!' they chorused eagerly.

'You're welcome!' the lady handed the bag to Charlie. 'Don't worry about the postcards, I'll put them back. And good luck with your project!'

'Wasn't that fantastic!' Charlie grinned when they got outside. 'We got our booklet of photos after all. And we've got enough money left for an ice cream each.'

She didn't say what was on her mind, that she was glad Alan didn't steal them. But she knew Alan was thinking that too.

The End

If you want to find out what happened to the vase, turn to page 70 and make another choice.

I'd rather look around the Hall first and get it over with,' Charlie pointed out. 'Then we'd have all afternoon to explore the grounds.'

Alan was dying to see the maze, but he agreed it made sense to get the boring bit over with. Then they could really enjoy themselves.

A guide came forward to greet them as they walked through the main entrance. 'Hello, you must be Charlie and Alan,' she smiled. 'The warden on the gate rang through to say you'd arrived.' She turned to Charlie. 'I met your father last week when he was working here. He said you're both doing a project about stately homes.'

'That's right,' Charlie nodded. She hadn't expected such a welcome! But then if children weren't usually allowed in unaccompanied she guessed it was only natural that the staff had been informed of her and Alan's arrival.

'Well, you're both just in time to join my tour,' the guide informed her. 'I'm sure you'll find it very interesting. And please don't hesitate to ask me if you have any questions.'

That was a piece of luck, Alan thought, as they both tagged onto the group of people waiting in the hall. Now the guide would show them around, pointing out all the important things, and all they had to do was make a few notes and take a few photos. They should be in the Hall an hour at the most, so they'd have bags of time to look around the grounds.

Turn to next page.

Charlie thought it would be a good idea to take a photo of the entrance hall. She took her camera out of her bag and focused on the winding staircase in the centre of the hall.

'I'm sorry, but you aren't allowed to take photographs inside the building,' the guide told her, pointing to a warning sign on the wall. 'However, you can buy a booklet of photos of the interior of Birbeck Hall in our souvenir shop for just over a pound. They'd be ideal for your project.'

'Sorry.' Charlie put away her camera, feeling an idiot for not noticing the sign.

The guide began the tour; first along the hall, then through the dining room, the drawing room and into yet another room. There was a lady or man on duty in every room. The guide told a curious Alan that they were room wardens whose job it was to keep an eye on things and answer any questions when the guide wasn't available. Although the rooms were huge, visitors could only walk within the rope barriers, which meant they could look at the old wooden furniture, dusty embroidered chairs, faded curtains and portraits of grim-faced ancestors but they couldn't touch them. As the guide talked about the paintings, the furniture, the people who had lived in the Hall, their families and friends, Charlie and Alan quickly scribbled notes of the things they wanted to include in their project.

Turn to page 32.

'They really get up my nose!' Alan glared after them. 'We've got to win the project this time and teach them a lesson. We've *got* to!'

'Maybe if we approach it from a different angle,' Charlie said thoughtfully. 'Dad's always on about that. He says everything's been done before so you have to approach it from a different angle to make it look different.'

'Yeah, like maybe we could get an interview with Lord and Lady Duncan,' Alan's imagination was really running away with him. 'Mr Cooper would love that! We'd win for sure!'

'Hey, that's quite a good idea . . . '

Both children discussed the idea as they walked towards the maze. It certainly had possibilities and they had to think of something different if they wanted to get one over Boffy and Jimbo. But they finally had to admit that people as important as Lord and Lady Duncan wouldn't bother to give an interview to a pair of schoolkids.

They had a great time in the maze. They played hide-and-seek, and chased each other down the narrow passageways. Then they pretended they were explorers as they tried to find their way out. When they finally came back out Jimbo and Boffy had gone.

'I bet they've gone to check out another stately home this afternoon,' grumbled Alan as they sat down at the same bench they had occupied to eat their sandwiches. 'Wouldn't surprise me if they don't visit Buckingham Palace too!'

Turn to next page.

Charlie grinned and opened her sandwiches. She wished she'd stopped at the corner shop now and got something else. She was starving! Still, she could get an ice-cream afterwards.

Then she noticed the carrier bag perched against the side of the bench.

'Someone's left this behind,' she said, picking up the bag and placing it on the table. She peered inside, expecting to see a plastic mac or sandwich wrappers and was surprised to find a black folder. She pulled out the folder. There was a big label on the front saying England's Heritage by Brian Brooks and James Shelton. 'It's Boffy and Jimbo's project!' she exclaimed, opening the folder and flicking through the pages. They were crammed full with notes and pictures of various stately homes. No wonder Boffy had looked so smug. They hadn't got a chance! 'Take a look at this,' she grimaced, handing it to Alan. 'We don't stand a chance with our project!'

Alan looked through it and groaned. 'Maybe we should just leave it here, then we might stand a chance of winning! Or maybe . . . ' he looked up at Charlie and grinned craftily. 'We could copy the notes ourselves, then our project would win!' he said triumphantly.

If you think they should copy Boffy and Jimbo's notes turn to page 9.

If you think they should leave the folder where it is, t
page 36.

If you think they should give them the folder bac
page 60.

As soon as the other visitors had disappeared around the corner, Alan stepped over the white chain. 'Come on!'

Charlie quickly glanced around, then followed him. They ran down the corridor, towards a door at the bottom.

'We'll only have a quick peep,' Alan said, going to the door directly in front of them and turning the handle. To his relief it wasn't locked.

'Quick! Get in!' he hissed.

They both stepped inside and looked around eagerly. To their disappointment it was just like a normal sitting room, except the furniture was old-fashioned, although a lot more comfortable than the furniture they'd seen in the other rooms. There were the usual paintings on the wall and a stuffed stag's head above a door on the opposite wall. It was a bit messy, though, as if Lord and Lady Duncan had gone out in a hurry. A couple of cupboard doors were flung open with some of the contents spilling onto the floor.

'Bit of a mess, isn't it?' remarked Charlie. 'I thought Lords and Ladies had maids to tidy up after them.'

'Maybe it's the maid's day off.' Alan glanced quickly around the room. 'It doesn't look much different to the rest of the house, does it?'

Charlie shook her head. 'I wonder what's in the other room?'

They both stared at the door, wondering whether to open it or not.

... look in the other room, turn to page

...ld join the rest of the group, turn to

Charlie decided to ignore Sita's look of reproach. She put the lion in her backpack, out of sight. Once they'd gone on a few rides Sita would soon forget about it.

But Sita didn't forget about it. Neither did Rashida. Although neither of them mentioned the lion again, the whole day was ruined. The easy, friendly manner they had earlier had gone, and now the children were all strained and tense with each other.

'Can we go home?' Sita asked after they had been on a couple of rides.

'I think we'd better, it's almost lunch-time,' Rashida agreed.

Charlie knew they weren't going home because they were hungry. They were going home because they were upset over the toy lion. They all walked home in silence. When they reached Mr Sharma's shop, Rashida turned to say goodbye.

'I probably won't have time to see you again, Charlie,' she said politely. 'We have a lot of relatives to visit and lots to do for the wedding. But it's been nice meeting you again.'

'Goodbye,' Charlie nodded. 'Goodbye Sita.'

Sita turned her reproachful look upon her. ''Bye,' she mumbled.

'I reckon I'll be going too,' Alan said. 'See you tomorrow, Charlie.'

Turn to next page.

Charlie had a lot to think about as she walked home. She wished she had never kept the lion. Breaking her promise had cost a friend. She felt really bad about hurting Rashida and Sita. But what was even worse was that she knew she had let Jesus down because she had broken a promise.

The End

If you want to see what happens if Charlie gives Sita the lion, turn to page 94 and make another choice.

'Yeah but the stuff's probably more expensive there,' Charlie reminded him. 'Anyway, I want one of those chocolate coconut bars Mr Sharma sells.'

They cycled down the road to the corner shop, propping their bikes against the wall outside before going in.

'Good morning!' Mr Sharma beamed at them. 'I have a surprise for you today, Charlie.' He turned towards the back of the shop and shouted, 'Rashida! Rashida! Come and see who is here!'

Charlie almost whooped with delight. 'Rashida's here?'

'Who's Rashida?' Alan asked curiously.

'I met her in Australia when I visited my cousins last Christmas. You know, I told you all about it. Mr Sharma's her uncle.'

'Charlie!' Rashida rushed into the shop and grinned at Charlie in delight. 'I was just coming to visit you!'

Both girls chatted excitedly, exchanging news. Rashida told Charlie that she had come over to England, with her parents, for her cousin Jaheed's wedding. They were staying with Mr Sharma, her father's brother, for two weeks. 'I was hoping we could go out somewhere today,' she said. 'Everyone is rushing around talking about the wedding and driving me mad!'

'And you are driving us mad, young lady,' Mr Sharma told her. 'I still have a shop to run, you know! Why don't you and your young friends go to the fair in the park? My treat, of course. That should keep you busy for the rest of the day.'

Turn to next page.

'Hey, that'd be unreal!' Rashida exclaimed, her eyes shining with excitement. 'You will come, won't you Charlie? And your friend, of course.'

Charlie hesitated and looked at Alan. 'Well, we were going to Birbeck Hall . . . '

'We can go tomorrow. We can use the tickets any day this week,' Alan reminded her quickly. He wasn't about to miss a day at the fair, especially when Rashida's uncle was paying for it, just to visit some crummy old house. 'Seeing as your friend has come all the way from Australia it's only right we should show her around a bit.' He grinned over at Rashida. 'I'm Alan, by the way. I live next door to Charlie.'

Rashida smiled. 'G'day Alan. Charlie's mentioned you in her letters.'

'Oh yes?' Alan raised an eyebrow questioningly at Charlie and she giggled.

'I only told her what a dope you were.'

'So you are going the fair – yes?' Mr Sharma asked.

'Yes, please!' The three children chorused together.

'Good.' Mr Sharma took some money out of his pocket and handed it to Rashida. 'This is for you all to spend.'

'Wow! Twenty pounds! Thanks, Uncle Ahmed.' Rashida smiled, pocketing the money. 'I'd better tell Mum where I'm going,' she told Charlie and Alan. 'I won't be long.'

'Actually, we'd better tell Nan and Alan's mum that we're not going to Birbeck Hall, after all,' Charlie suddenly remembered.

'And we won't need our bikes,' Alan pointed out.

'See you in a few minutes then!' Rashida called, running behind the counter to the back of the shop.

Turn to page 38.

'Alan! Charlie! It's okay, I've found her!' Rashida was running towards them, her face lit up with relief, firmly clasping Sita's hand in hers.

Alan and Charlie whooped with joy. They'd never been so glad to see anyone in their entire life!

'She was standing by the ice-cream hut,' Rashida told them. 'She said she got fed up of waiting so went to see what ice-cream she wanted!'

'And you still haven't bought me one!' Sita retorted. It was obvious she couldn't understand what all the fuss was about.

'I'm not sure you deserve one,' Rashida told her. 'We've all been worried sick. It was really naughty of you to go off by yourself like that!'

'I didn't go off!' Sita pouted. 'I was waiting for you by the ice-cream stand!'

'But I told you to wait here, didn't I?' Rashida was torn between wanting to hug her little sister and wanting to throttle her!

'Rashida's right, you shouldn't have gone off like that,' Charlie said. 'But we shouldn't have left you on your own either. So we were all to blame.'

'So how about if we all have an ice-cream and then find some rides that we can all go on?' suggested Alan. 'I wouldn't want to go through the last twenty minutes again, so from now on we all stick together. Right?'

And they all agreed with that.

The End

'There's only one way to find out.' Alan ran across the room, opened the door – and gasped. The scene that met his eyes was like something out of a detective movie. In the middle of the room a dark-haired, bearded man was gagged and tied, hands behind his back, to a chair while one masked man was robbing a wall safe and another masked man was rummaging through a wooden bureau in the corner of the room.

'What's up?' Charlie's eyes widened as she peered over her friend's shoulder into the room.

'Burglars!' hissed Alan. 'We'd better go and get help!'

But it was too late. The masked man had now finished searching through the bureau and as he turned around he spotted the two children watching him. 'You kids, get in here, quick!' he shouted, pointing the gun at them. 'And no funny moves!'

They wouldn't dare – not with a gun pointing at them! Raising their hands in the air, Charlie and Alan slowly entered the room.

Turn to page 49.

They both knelt down and watched for a moment, sheltered by the trees, as the men piled the furniture into the van. Every few seconds the men would look around shiftily, as if making sure no one was watching. Charlie was sure they were thieves. Alan was thinking the same thing. He quickly scribbled the registration number of the van down onto his note pad.

'What shall we do?' Charlie whispered.

'Well, we can't tackle them ourselves, that's for sure,' Alan replied. He wasn't going to be a mug. If the men were thieves they were probably armed and extremely dangerous. 'We'd better go and tell someone, before they get away!'

Suddenly a dark shadow fell over them. Their hearts pounded as they looked up into the face of a third man. He was large and rather fierce-looking. He grabbed them both by the shoulders and pulled them up off their knees. 'What are you kids doing here?' he boomed.

He must be the look-out man! Alan thought fast. 'Sorry, we didn't realise we were trespassing on private property. We were trying to find the railway.'

The man released his grip and for a moment it seemed like he was going to let them go, then a dark frown crossed his forehead as he stared down at the notebook in Alan's hand.

Turn to next page.

'You're lying, kid!' he growled furiously.

'Hey, what's going on?' one of the men shouted over from the van. 'What are those kids doing here?'

'Snooping!' snarled the first man, dragging Charlie and Alan over to the van. 'This smart alec here has even written down the number of our van!'

'What are we going to do with the little brats?' asked the other man.

The first man thought for a moment and then decided, 'We'd better take them with us, we haven't got time to hang about!'

Then, to Charlie and Alan's horror they were thrust into the back of the van and the door slammed firmly shut.

Turn to page 51.

One look at their anxious faces and Charlie knew she couldn't do it. Boffy and Jimbo might be a pair of creeps but cheating was wrong.

'Yes, we did,' she nodded. 'We were going to bring it around to you later.'

Alan had been walking up the path as she spoke and she saw a frown crease across his forehead as he heard her remarks. He wasn't too pleased, but she knew she was doing the right thing. Boffy and Jimbo's look of relief proved that.

'Hang on and I'll go and get it for you,' she said.

'Thanks! We don't know what we'd have done if you hadn't found it!' Boffy's gratitude made her feel bad that she had even considered copying the project.

'Ah well, we still might win with our project,' Alan said with a shrug when Boffy and Jimbo had left. They had both been so delighted that their precious project wasn't lost after all, that he had to admit Charlie had been right to hand it back.

'And if we don't, it won't be the end of the world!' Charlie said. 'I'm just glad we did the right thing. If we win this project I want it to be fair and square!'

And Alan agreed with that.

The End

As they walked toward the library, Alan noticed a white chain sectioning off another corridor, which led to several rooms. A notice on the wall said 'Private'.

'That's Lord and Lady Duncan's private quarters,' the guide said, noticing Alan's look of curiosity. 'They have modernised the interior of the west wing of the house and made it their home.'

'You mean they really live here?' Charlie shot a quick look down the corridor, hoping to see someone come out of one of the rooms. She had never seen a real Lord or Lady before.

The guide smiled. 'They certainly do. And if they're at home they often come out to greet visitors. But I'm afraid they're both out today.'

Charlie sighed. She would have loved to have met them. It would have been ace if they could have written in their project that they'd actually met Lord and Lady Duncan.

The guide was carrying on around the corner now, telling the group about the paintings lining the hall. Alan grabbed Charlie's arm as she went to follow them. 'Hang on,' he whispered.

Turn to page 43.

'It's OK kids, you're safe now!'

It took them a moment to focus and by that time the strong arms of two policemen were helping them out of the van. They were safe! But how?

'How did you find us?' Charlie's voice was barely a whisper. She still couldn't believe they were actually safe.

'Lady Duncan came home early and found her husband tied up in their apartment. A lot of their furniture had been taken, and some other valuables from the Hall. We searched the grounds for clues and found this notebook lying on the ground, right by some van tyre marks.' The policeman held up Alan's notebook with the van's registration number written in large letters on the cover, below Alan's name and address. 'We checked out the address and found Alan's mum worried because you were both supposed to be home by four o'clock and hadn't turned up yet. Then we checked the registration number and discovered that the van had been stolen. We guessed it had been used for the robbery and put out an alert to all patrol cars to keep an eye out for it.' He smiled. 'Good job you dropped that notebook, eh kids?'

'It sure was!' Alan and Charlie smiled happily at each other. God had answered their prayers, after all.

The End

If you want to know what happens if they got to the maze first, turn to page 40 and make another choice.

Alan paid for the postcards. He grinned at Charlie as they walked out of the shop and she smiled back. It was silly of her to panic like that. They'd got the booklet now and no one was any the wiser.

But as soon as they stepped out of the door, someone grabbed their arms.

'Just a moment, you two!'

Charlie gasped, her heart thudding. They'd been caught!

She turned around fearfully to face a fair-haired, stern-looking lady. A quick glance at Alan showed Charlie that he was just as nervous as she was.

'Yes?' Alan squeaked.

'I think you'd both better come with me and explain why you've put that booklet in your pocket without paying for it!' the woman said.

Charlie licked her lips and glanced nervously around the shop, hoping no one was watching them. To her horror she saw two of their classmates, Boffy Brookes and Jimbo, grinning over at her. Oh no! They must have just come in and judging by the triumphant look on their faces they knew exactly what was going on. Now it would be all around school. And what was worse, their mothers were with them and Mrs Brookes was the worst gossip going – it wouldn't be long before the news that Charlie and Alan had been caught shoplifting got back to their parents.

Turn to next page.

The lady marched them both to a security guard who gave then a stern warning and told them to leave the premises immediately. Charlie and Alan felt sick. Now they would have to go back and tell their parents before Mrs Brookes told them. Charlie was dreading that. She knew she had let her father down badly, after he'd gone to so much trouble to get them complimentary tickets. And what was worse she had let Jesus down too.

The End

They both looked at each other, then, without saying a word, Alan put the bag down on the ground.

'Come on, let's go and catch the railway and have a ride around the grounds,' he said.

Charlie followed him. Boffy and Jimbo had only themselves to blame, they shouldn't have been so careless.

It was a great afternoon. They even got to see a couple of deer! Laughing and chattering, they set off back through the wood to the Hall. That was the only place they had left to see now.

As they came out of the wood, Charlie saw a rolled up bundle of paper on the road and frowned. She hated to see litter lying around. It was her pet hate. 'Honestly, why can't people use the bins!' she grumbled, picking it up. But she could see now that it wasn't a bundle of paper, it was more like a piece of cloth. Carefully she unrolled it and gasped at the painting of a horse she unveiled. 'Fancy someone throwing this away,' she said. 'It's lovely!'

'Looks pretty old to me,' Alan remarked. 'Nice horse, though.'

'You know, I don't think it's been thrown away, it looks too valuable,' Charlie said. 'I'm sure it's one of the paintings from the Hall.'

Alan agreed with her. 'But what's it doing here?' he asked.

Charlie shook her head. 'I don't know. But I think we'd better hand it in when we get to the Hall.' She rolled the painting up and put it in her backpack.

Turn to next page.

As soon as they entered the Hall, Charlie handed the painting to the lady at the reception desk. 'We found this on the road at the back of the Hall and were wondering if it came from here,' she said.

The lady took the painting off her and unrolled it. 'It certainly does!' she gasped. 'Where exactly did you find it?'

She listened intently as Charlie explained, then reached for the telephone. 'Thank you very much for returning the painting to us,' she said as she dialled. 'Perhaps you would like to carry on with your tour of the Hall while I find out what the painting was doing in the grounds.'

Charlie and Alan nodded and set off to look around the Hall. They only had time for a quick tour because they'd promised to be home by four. But they managed to take enough notes for their project and decided to cut a few pictures out of the guide book, and with the photos they'd taken of the grounds they were sure they would have enough. All in all, they both agreed, it had been an enjoyable day.

Turn to page 86.

Nan was out shopping, so Alan's mother promised to let her know about the change of plan.

When the two children returned to the corner shop, they found Rashida waiting for them with a little girl of about five in tow. 'Mum said I have to take Sita too. I hope you don't mind?' she said.

Actually, Charlie and Alan did mind but neither of them liked to say so. If they had to keep an eye on a young kid they wouldn't be able to have as much fun. Still, it was a small price to pay for a free day at the fair and it was hardly Rashida's fault if she had to take her kid sister along. 'No, of course not!' Charlie smiled reassuringly. Alan nodded in agreement.

'Well, let's split the money before we go,' Rashida said. 'Twenty pounds between four of us, that's five pounds each.' She handed Charlie and Alan a five pound note each.

'Thanks!' They both said, thinking how nice it was of Rashida to share the money out instead of lording it over them by paying for everything when they got to the fair.

The park was only a few minutes walk away, and the fair was held at the far end. They could see some of the rides and hear the music and squeals of excitement long before they got there.

'I want to go on that big ride!' shouted Sita, her eyes shining with delight as she pointed to the Big Wheel towering above the other rides.

Turn to next page.

'Don't be silly, you can't go on that – it's much too dangerous!' Rashida told her. 'You have to go on the little rides that go round and round, not up in the air.'

'I'm not a baby!' protested Sita. 'I'm at school now!'

'Maybe, but you're still not big enough to go on that, and that's that!' Rashida told her firmly.

Alan was eyeing up the Big Wheel too. 'I'd like to have a go on it,' he said. 'Anyone else coming?'

'You bet!' Charlie said enthusiastically.

'I'd like to but what about Sita?' asked Rashida. 'She's much too young.'

'I am not!' Sita protested indignantly.

'Yes you are!' Rashida looked over at Alan and Charlie. 'You two go on the ride and I'll wait with Sita.'

Turn to page 44.

'Let me see,' Charlie took the guide book off him and scanned the page. 'Oh, look, there's deer and horses in the parkland at the back of the house!' she squealed excitedly. She loved animals. 'I've got to see them!'

'Come on then, we can have a look around the house later!' Alan was already heading for the path along the side of the Hall.

'Hey, where are you going?' called Charlie, running after him. 'The deer and horses are at the *back* of the house!'

'I know, but if we go around the maze first, we can take the railway around the rest of the park,' Alan told her.

If you think they should go to the maze first, turn to page 14.
If you think they should see the deer and horses first, turn to page 74.

For a moment Charlie was tempted. Then she shook her head. 'No, we can't do that, it would be trespassing.'

'But no one would know if we were real quick,' Alan told her.

'Maybe not, but it's wrong to sneak into other people's private rooms,' Charlie reminded him. 'Anyway, we'd know. And so would God.'

Alan groaned, he hated it when Charlie said things like that. But he knew she was right.

They ran along the corridor and around the corner to join the rest of the group who were still in the library.

'Ah, there you are,' smiled the guide. 'I was wondering where you two had gone. Something caught your eye, did it?'

Charlie and Alan nodded, both thinking that it was a good job they hadn't trespassed into the private quarters. The guide might have come looking for them and then they would have been in trouble!

When they had finished the tour of the ground floor they went up the spiral staircase to the second floor. As they turned at the top Charlie glanced down. Two women were in the hall looking at the paintings. Shame they missed the guided tour, Charlie thought. They seemed really interested in the things, they were studying everything so intently. One woman was actually leaning over the barrier rail and touching things even though the guide had said no one was to touch anything. Just like grown-ups to think they could do what they wanted, she thought. Now if she or Alan touched anything they'd be in mega trouble!

Turn to next page.

'Come on, slow coach! The others are way ahead!' Alan called.

'Coming!' Charlie glanced idly back downstairs again. The women had now gone. Then she frowned. She was sure there had been a vase on that cupboard in the corner, and now it was missing!

Turn to page 70.

'What's up?' She turned to him, puzzled.

'If we wait until the others have gone we could take a look down there,' Alan nodded towards the private quarters.

'You've got to be kidding! That's trespassing! We'll be in mega trouble if anyone catches us!'

'Nobody will know. The guide just said that Lord and Lady Duncan are out for the day,' Alan reminded her. 'And it would be brill if we could put something about their private quarters in our project.'

If you think they should take a look at the private quarters, turn to page 22.
If you think they shouldn't, turn to page 41.

Charlie and Alan could see that Rashida really wanted to go on the Big Wheel as well. They had known that bringing Sita's kid sister along would spoil the fun. Fancy having to miss out on the best ride at the fair!

'Can't you tell her to wait for you? We won't be long,' suggested Alan. 'She can stand by the ticket office and watch.'

Rashida hesitated. She really did want to go on the ride with her friends, but should she leave Sita on her own?

Charlie was thinking the same thing. Maybe she should offer to stay with Sita while Rashida went on the big wheel with Alan, she thought. But that meant she would miss the ride.

If you think Rashida should tell Sita to wait for them, turn to page 96.
If you think Rashida should wait with Sita and miss the ride, turn to page 88.
If you think Charlie should offer to wait with Sita and let Rashida go on the ride, turn to page 61.

'Did you all have a nice time?' Mr Sharma asked when they arrived back at the shop.

'Excellent!' Rashida told him. 'Thank you for treating us, Uncle Ahmed.'

'Yes, thank you. It was very kind of you,' Charlie and Alan quickly added their thanks.

'You are most welcome,' Mr Sharma beamed.

'We'll see you tomorrow, Rashida,' Charlie told her friend.

'No, I have to visit relatives tomorrow,' Rashida told her. 'Perhaps you can stay for tea tonight instead? You too, of course, Alan,' she added politely.

Alan shook his head. He had enjoyed Charlie and Rashida's company at the fair but didn't fancy spending a whole evening listening to girl talk. Besides he was sure Rashida and Charlie had a lot of news to catch up on about Charlie's cousins and their friends in Australia and he'd only feel in the way. 'Thanks, but I think I'll leave you to it. Perhaps I'll see you at the weekend, Rashida. Thanks again for treating us to the fair, Mr Sharma.' He waved and left.

'You'll stop for tea, won't you, Charlie?' Rashida begged.

'I'd love too, if that's okay?' Charlie looked at Mr Sharma.

'Certainly. You are most welcome,' he assured her.

'Great, well I'll just go and ask Nan. I'm sure she won't mind.'

Nan didn't mind at all. She had heard Charlie talk about Rashida and was delighted that she had come over for a visit. 'I'd love to meet Rashida and her family,' she told Charlie. 'Ask them if they would all like to come to tea on Saturday.'

'Thanks, Nan. I will,' Charlie smiled.

Turn to page 81.

They both decided not to risk it.

'It'd probably be just as boring as this room, anyway,' said Alan.

Charlie wasn't too sure about that. She'd have loved to open the other door to see if that room was more interesting. But she knew it was wrong. They'd trespassed enough already.

'I guess we'd better go back before the guide realises we're missing,' she said.

They hurried out of the room and along the corridor. To their dismay, the guide was walking down towards them.

'What are you children doing?' she asked sternly. 'I told you these were the private quarters of Lord and Lady Duncan.' Then she frowned. 'That's strange, the alarm should have gone off as soon as you set foot in that corridor – I'd better check why it didn't work.'

'Probably because the door isn't locked,' volunteered Alan.

Now the guard looked really worried. 'What! Y-you've been *inside* the apartment?' she demanded.

'I'm sorry, we didn't mean to do anything wrong,' Charlie apologized. 'We just wanted to see what their rooms were like. We didn't touch anything honest!'

'Yeah, we only had a quick peep and then we came back out,' Alan assured her.

Turn to next page.

But the guide had already run into the next room, where she whispered something to the room warden then ran off down the hall as if her life depended upon it.

The room warden came out into the corridor, told Charlie and Alan to follow her, and hurried off to join the rest of the group who were still in the library. 'I'm sorry, but I'm afraid I'll have to ask you all to come back to the entrance hall for a few minutes,' she announced.

'I wonder what's going on?' Charlie said curiously as the room warden led them all back to the hall, where they found three security guards in earnest discussion with the guide.

'I bet there's been a burglary!' Alan's eyes were shining with excitement. 'That's why the door wasn't locked and the room was in such a mess!'

'Don't be daft, there's too many people around!' scoffed Charlie. 'Anyway, who'd want to break into a place like this!'

But when the police arrived not long afterwards, she had to admit that Alan was probably right.

'Just think, if we hadn't gone into the room no one would have known about it until that Lord and his wife came home,' she said excitedly.

Everyone else was saying the same thing, they were all crowding around Charlie and Alan, asking them to describe what they had seen in the room. Even the guide seemed to have forgiven them for trespassing.

To everyone's surprise, when the police returned, they had two handcuffed prisoners with them.

Turn to next page.

'We caught them in the act!' one of the policemen told the guide. 'Robbing the safe, they were. Can you call a doctor for Lord Duncan? We found him tied up and gagged, with a nasty bruise on his head. He seems OK but it's best to get him checked out.'

'Lord Duncan! But he was supposed to be out for the day!' gasped the guide.

Charlie and Alan looked at each other in alarm. The thieves had still been in the apartment when they had sneaked in. And Lord Duncan was their prisoner. If they had gone into the other room they probably would have ended up being captured too! They both went a bit pale as they thought of the lucky escape they had had. Thank goodness they hadn't trespassed any further!

Turn to page 59.

'Just what we need, a couple of meddling kids!' The man emptying the wall safe groaned. 'What are we going to do with them?'

'Tie 'em up, like his lordship,' sneered the other man. 'OK, kids, get up against this wall! And make it snappy!' He beckoned with his gun towards the far wall.

Charlie and Alan looked at each other nervously. They knew they had to do what the man with the gun said so they slowly walked across the room to the wall. After ordering them both to sit down, back to back, the man tied their hands together and gagged them.

'Ready?' the other man had now emptied the safe and was obviously anxious to go.

'Yep. Let's get out of here!' The man with the gun grabbed his bag off the floor, then both men ran out of the room, shutting the door behind them.

Turn to page 95.

Charlie and Alan were really excited when the police telephoned a couple of hours later to tell them that one of the photos Charlie had taken from the railway showed the van driving along the road, and what was even better they'd managed to enlarge the photo enough to reveal part of the registration number. Charlie and Alan couldn't believe that they had provided evidence to help catch the thieves! Their day at Birbeck Hall had turned out to be quite an adventure, after all!

The End

If you want to know what would have happened if they had gone to the shops first, turn to page 8 and make another choice.

It was dark inside the van. Both children sat close together, hugging their knees to try and stop themselves shaking with fear.

'What are we gonna do now?' Alan hissed.

'There's only one thing we can do,' Charlie told him. 'Pray!'

She shut her eyes and prayed quietly. 'Please Lord show us what to do. Help us get away from these men. Thank you. Amen.'

For once, Alan joined in with her. He always felt a bit uncomfortable when Charlie went on about God and praying but right now he decided that God was about the only one who could help them.

Turn to page 85.

'One of the room wardens has probably moved the vase and put it somewhere else,' said Alan. 'Come on, let's catch the others up. If we don't get a move on we won't have time to see the grounds.'

'I guess you're right,' Charlie agreed. Both children hurried along the hall to catch up with the group of visitors who were now about to go into a bedroom.

'This is known as the Blue Bedroom,' the guide was telling them. 'Note the four-poster bed which was carved in . . . '

Alan and Charlie each took a notepad out of their pockets and started scribbling down what the guide was saying. They needed as much information as possible if they wanted to win the prize for their project.

Turn to page 56.

Alan glanced unconcernedly over at the van. 'They're probably taking it to be cleaned or something. Antiques need special treatment, don't they?'

Charlie had to admit that made sense. As if thieves would load up a van with valuable antiques in broad daylight! Her imagination was running away with her again.

Alan returned to studying the map. 'I've figured out where we went wrong,' he said. 'You were holding the map upside down so we turned right instead of left.'

Charlie felt a right wally!

They turned back into the wood and soon found the turning that lead to the railway. They couldn't believe their luck when they saw that the train was in. They ran over to join the other people piling into the trucks and quickly climbed into an empty carriage at the back. A few seconds later the train set off.

Turn to the next page.

The railway went right around the grounds, chugging slowly enough for them to admire and take photos of the wonderful flower gardens, the peacocks strutting across the lawns and the big, rambling house in the middle of it all.

After the railway ride, they ate their sandwiches while walking around the maze, which luckily was signposted or they'd have never got out!

'Oh no, look at the time!' Charlie gasped, glancing at her watch. 'It's half past two already and we haven't even looked around the Hall yet.' She couldn't believe the day had gone so fast. If they wanted to be home by four – they'd be grounded for the rest of the week if they didn't get back on time – they'd better get a move on!

Unfortunately, they had just missed the guided tour of the Hall, but the room wardens were only too pleased to give them any information they wanted. So they arrived home with plenty of notes for their project, agreeing to meet up at Charlie's house later that evening to write them up.

Turn to page 68.

It was no good, she couldn't keep it. If she did the whole day would be ruined. Plus Rashida probably wouldn't want to know her anymore. And no cuddly toy animal was worth losing a friend over. Charlie swallowed her pride as Sita and Rashida joined them. She bent down and handed the lion to the little girl.

'I'm sorry, Sita, I didn't mean to be selfish. I did promise you could have the prize so of course the lion is yours.' She straightened up and quickly turned away so she couldn't seek the look of scorn on the others' faces.

'Thank you!' Sita flung her arms around Charlie's waist. 'This will be my best toy ever!' She beamed, all resentment forgotten. Then she whispered. 'I don't blame you for not wanting to give it up, I wouldn't have wanted to either!'

Rashida and Alan burst out laughing and Charlie joined them. The moment of awkwardness was forgotten. Charlie had done the right thing and that was all that mattered.

'Come on then, Charlie. Let's show these two how to drive!' shouted Alan.

They all ran, laughing, over to the dodgem cars. They were going to have the best day ever!

The End

The tour of Birbeck Hall ended with a visit to the souvenir shop. Charlie and Alan looked around at the array of maps, books, pencils, notebooks, postcards, picture boxes of fudge and various ornaments that filled the shop.

'Hey, these are excellent!' Alan held up an eraser in the shape of Birbeck Hall; he collected erasers. 'They're only 75p.'

'Mm,' Charlie said absently, busy looking at the various animal figures. She didn't share Alan's passion for collecting erasers but she did collect cuddly toys. She picked up a cuddly red squirrel that would look great with the kangaroo she brought back from her holiday in Australia last year. It was four pounds twenty-five and she only had four pounds fifty left now they had bought the guide book. That meant she could only afford to buy it if she didn't have an ice-cream or anything else. She looked at the squirrel again. It was worth it. Who needed ice-cream anyway? She went to the till and proudly handed over the money. The lady smiled and put the squirrel in a paper bag. 'Lovely aren't they?' she said.

Alan was clutching the eraser, a pen and pencil and a notebook, all bearing a picture of Birbeck Hall. It all came to three pounds forty-five pence. Charlie thought the squirrel was much better value.

It wasn't until they left the shop that Charlie remembered the photos for their project. They were going to buy the little book that the guide had mentioned to them. Maybe Alan had enough money left.

Turn to next page.

He hadn't. 'Mum gave me four pounds fifty, so I've only got fifty-five pence left,' he told her.

'And I've got twenty-five – so that makes eighty pence all together,' she sighed. 'Oh well, we should be able to get a couple of postcards or something for that.'

They went back into the shop and walked over to the stand of postcards, studying them carefully. 'We don't need any of the outside of the house, we can take some photos of it,' Charlie pointed out as Alan picked one up.

'There's a couple here of different rooms,' Alan put the postcard back and picked up one of the library. 'They're 15p each so we could buy five. Hey, here's the photo book the guide was on about.' He took a booklet off the rail and opened it out to reveal a long concertina of card showing about a dozen photos of the interior of Birbeck Hall. 'Wow, these are ace!'

'Brill!' Charlie agreed. 'How much is it?'

Alan flipped over the card to glance at the price. '£1.25,' he sighed. 'We're 45p short.'

Both children looked at each other disappointedly. The booklet would have been ideal for their project. If only they could have it.

Turn to next page.

Maybe they could have it. Alan looked around cautiously. The lady on the till was serving someone and the few other people in the shop were busy looking for souvenirs, no one was bothering with them. It would be really easy to sneak the booklet in his pocket. No one would know.

'We could nick it,' he whispered to Charlie. 'No one's looking.'

'What?' Charlie stared incredulously at him.

If you think they should steal the booklet, turn to page 87.
If you think they should make do with a couple of the postcards, turn to page 16.

Luckily, apart from the bruise on his head, Lord Duncan was unhurt. He was so grateful to Charlie and Alan for their part in capturing the thieves that he asked them to come to tea on Sunday, promising them a full tour of his private quarters, and lots of personal photos and information for their project. Charlie and Alan were delighted. With that sort of information they were bound to win the prize! But even better than that, they were actually having tea with a real Lord and Lady! Just wait until the rest of the kids in the class knew about that!

The End

Charlie knew Jesus wouldn't want her to cheat. 'I'd love to win the prize and take Boffy and Jimbo down a peg or two,' she told Alan. 'But it wouldn't be right to copy their work. We've got to give them the folder back.'

Alan thought about it and agreed. They wanted to win the prize, but not that way.

On the way home they stopped off at Boffy's to return the project. He and Jimbo were really pleased to get it back. They had thought all their hard work was lost for good. They were so pleased they let Charlie and Alan have some photos of stately homes that they didn't need themselves.

Charlie and Alan were really pleased too. They had done the right thing. And now they were going to have a bash at doing the best project ever. Maybe they'd win, maybe they wouldn't. But at least if they did win they'd know they had done it fair and square.

The End

'You and Alan go on the ride, I'll wait with Sita,' Charlie offered. 'We'll take a look at the hoopla stall, over there.'

'Are you sure?' Rashida asked.

''Course. Go on!'

'Hurry up, it'll be starting in a minute!' Alan shouted.

'Thanks!' Rashida smiled gratefully and ran over to join Alan in the queue.

'Come on Sita, let's see if we can win a prize on the hoopla stall,' Charlie held out her hand to the little girl.

Sita clasped her hand eagerly. 'You mean a prize for me?' she asked. 'Can I keep it? Promise?'

''Course you can keep it,' Charlie smiled at her. 'But we might not win so don't sulk if we don't, will you?'

'I won't,' Sita promised. 'But I hope we do. Winning a prize would be much better than going on the Big Wheel.'

'It sure would!' grinned Charlie.

Turn to page 93.

That seemed to worry Rashida even more. Her eyes widened in alarm. 'So you *do* think someone's kidnapped her!' she cried.

'Hey, cool it!' Alan sounded calmer than he felt. 'There's no need to freak out. We don't even know if the kid is missing yet! She's probably just wandered off to have a look around that's all. Let's have a look for her ourselves before we do anything drastic like calling the police.'

Charlie had to agree that made sense. But she knew they couldn't leave it too long before telling the policeman.

'Okay, we'll all split up and have a look around. We'll meet back here in fifteen minutes and if we haven't found Sita we'll go and tell a policeman,' she suggested. 'Everyone agree?'

Rashida nodded numbly. Many a time she had felt like murdering her little sister, but right now she'd give anything to see her cheeky face again.

Turn to next page.

Exactly fifteen minutes later, Charlie arrived back at the Big Wheel. She waited anxiously for the others to join her. She knew that if they hadn't found Sita then they had to tell the police fast. Poor Rashida must be going mad with worry. They should never have left Sita on her own, it was stupid and selfish of them. Oh, God, please let Alan or Rashida find Sita. Please God, she prayed desperately.

'There's no sign of the kid anywhere,' Alan looked anxious as he joined her. 'Let's hope Rashida has had better luck.'

'Oh, Alan, what are we going to do?' Charlie was near to tears. 'She's only a little kid and she's in a strange country too! We should all have had more sense . . . '

'I know! I know!' Alan cut her short. He'd been telling himself the same things for the past fifteen minutes.

Turn to page 27.

Charlie and Alan worked hard on the project all week. They were quite pleased with their efforts. They ended up only copying a few pages of Boffy and Jimbo's notes, and using half a dozen of their pictures, so they managed to persuade themselves that the project was all their own work.

Mr Cooper was pleased with it too, and awarded them first prize – a walkie-talkie set. Boffy and Jimbo had managed to put another project together and got second prize of a £5 book voucher.

'You two have obviously worked very hard on this project,' Mr Cooper told Charlie and Alan. 'Well done!'

They both went out to break, glowing with pride.

But when they came back into the classroom they found Boffy and Jimbo looking through their project.

'Just as I thought, you *did* find our project!' Boffy said accusingly. 'You copied our notes – and took our pictures!'

'You're nothing but a pair of cheats!' glared Jimbo.

'What's going on here?' demanded Mr Cooper. He had come into the classroom just in time to hear the accusations. 'I think you two had better explain those remarks!'

Boffy and Jimbo told him about losing their project folder at Birbeck Hall. 'They found it and copied our notes, Sir!' Boffy told him.

'We didn't, Sir!' denied Charlie and Alan.

'Yes you did and I can prove it!' Boffy smirked at them triumphantly. 'That photo's my mum's. She took it when she visited Gladleigh Manor last year.' He pointed to the figure of a woman in a blue coat standing by the entrance. 'And that's my Aunt Sarah!'

Turn to next page.

Charlie and Alan looked at each other nervously. Now they were for it. If only they had handed the folder back when they found it. They had known it was wrong to cheat. Now they were going to be in mega trouble. They'd have to hand their prize back and by the look on Mr Cooper's face he was planning on giving them detention and extra homework for the rest of the year!

The End

If you want to know what would have happened if they'd handed the folder back, turn to page 21 and make another choice.

'We'll start with the kiddies' rides,' the policeman said as they walked back towards the fair. 'Your sister could have wandered off to take a look at them.'

'She likes the Ghost Train,' Rashida said. 'Maybe . . . there she is!' she shrieked. 'Alan's found her!'

Sure enough, Alan and Sita were running towards them. Rashida raced across and hugged her sister, saying how glad she was to have found her, and scolding her for going off, all at the same time. Charlie smiled happily. She felt like hugging and scolding Sita too!

The policeman grinned in relief and radioed a message that the missing girl had been found safe and well.

'I'm sorry, we've wasted your time,' Charlie told him.

'You haven't wasted my time at all, love. You were right to come and tell me as soon as the little girl disappeared. That's what I'm here for.' The policeman replied. 'The main thing is that she's been found safe and sound.'

Then he walked over to Alan, Rashida and Sita. 'Well done, lad,' he said to Alan. 'Where did you find her?'

'By the ice-cream hut,' Alan grinned. 'We'd promised her an ice-cream when we came off the Big Wheel so she went to see what kind she wanted.'

'I wasn't lost!' Sita protested to the policeman.

'I'm glad to hear it,' the policeman smiled. 'But don't go wandering off again without your sister, OK?'

'OK!' Sita nodded solemnly.

Turn to next page.

The policeman looked at Rashida, Alan and Charlie. 'And I don't think I need to tell you three never to leave a youngster on their own again, do I?'

'No way!' Rashida assured him. 'From now on if Sita can't go on the ride, I don't either.'

And they all agreed with that.

The End

'What did you think of the Hall?' Charlie's dad asked when he came home from work that night. 'Pretty impressive, isn't it?'

Charlie nodded. 'I don't think I'd like to live in a place like that though, I prefer it here.'

Dad grinned. 'So do I!'

'Alan's here!' Nan called from the kitchen.

Charlie looked over at Dad. 'OK if we work on our project down here? It's a bit cold upstairs.'

'Sure, I'll even give you a hand if you like, when I've watched the news.' He switched over the TV channels and settled down to drink his cup of tea and watch the news.

Alan came in, carrying his notebooks, some sheets of paper and a pen. 'Mum's taking my film in to be developed tomorrow, so we can sort out the photos at the weekend,' he said.

Charlie went to agree when a sudden gasp from Dad made her look over at him. He had turned the volume up on the TV and was leaning forward on his seat, listening intently. Charlie caught the name Birbeck Hall and a photo of a white van was flashed onto the screen. 'What's up?' she asked.

'Seems like there was a robbery at Birbeck Hall this afternoon, and that white van was the getaway vehicle,' Dad told her. 'Quite a lot of stuff was taken apparently. Thank goodness you kids weren't caught up in it!'

Charlie was staring at the van. 'That's the one we saw,' she said slowly. 'It was parked at the back of the Hall and some men were putting furniture in it.' She turned to Alan. 'So those men *were* thieves!'

Turn to next page.

'You mean you saw something?' Dad asked.

Charlie nodded. Quickly, she and Alan told him what they had seen that afternoon. As soon as they'd finished, her father reached for the phone. 'I think the police will be interested in this,' he told them.

He was right. The police were very interested. Charlie and Alan described the van and the men in it as well as they could. Then the police sergeant asked them if they'd taken any photos.

'We took some of the horses, and some when we were on the railway,' Alan told him.

The policeman nodded thoughtfully. 'We'd like to develop the film in our lab,' he said. 'You never know, there could be something on it.'

Turn to page 50.

'Are you comin' or not?' Alan was getting impatient.

Charlie was still staring downstairs. 'That vase has gone!'

Alan looked down, puzzled. 'What vase?'

'The vase that was on that little cupboard in the hall. Two women were looking at it and now the vase has gone! I reckon they've stolen it.'

Alan frowned. He couldn't remember seeing a vase on the cupboard. 'Are you sure?'

'They must have done, it's gone!' Charlie was indignant. 'Don't you remember, the guide told us that the first Lord Duncan brought it home from China as a present for his wife. She said it was really valuable.' She turned to him, her eyes wide with shock. 'We can't let them get away with it! We've got to tell the guide!'

Alan looked at her doubtfully. He couldn't really remember seeing the vase, he'd been too interested in the stuffed animals in glass cases to bother with anything else. But Charlie seemed positive.

'Are you sure?' he asked cautiously. 'You can't go around accusing people of stealing things unless you're sure.'

He was right, Charlie thought. Calling someone a thief was a serious thing. What was it that Mrs Francis, their RE teacher, had said last week about jumping to conclusions and judging people falsely?

If you think they should tell the guide about the missing vase, turn to page 77.
If you think they should do nothing, turn to page 52.

'We'd better tell the policeman,' Rashida said tearfully. 'We've got to find Sita quickly. We've *got* to!'

Charlie put a comforting arm around her friend's shoulder. 'Don't worry, we'll find her.'

'Tell you what. You two go and tell the policeman and I'll have a look for Sita around the fair,' suggested Alan.

They all agreed that this made sense, so the two girls raced off to find the policeman. They knew there was no time to lose if they wanted to find Sita safe and sound.

Luckily, the policeman was still patrolling by the gates.

'My little sister is missing!' Rashida gasped as they ran over to him. 'Please can you help us find her?'

The policeman listened to their breathless story, carefully writing down a description of Sita.

'OK, now don't worry, we'll find your sister,' he told Rashida. He switched on his radio and reported briefly what had happened, giving Sita's description and asking for someone to keep an eye on all the park entrances.

'Why do you want someone to watch the entrances. Do you think someone's kidnapped her?' wailed Rashida.

'Well, it's a possibility so it's best to take precautions. Another possibility is that your sister may leave the park herself and try and find her way home. But I reckon she's probably wandered off to have a look at the rides,' the policeman said reassuringly. 'So let's take a look around, shall we?'

Turn to next page.

Another policeman was walking over to them.

'I'll take over, Don, while you look for the kid,' he offered. 'How old is she?'

'Five,' replied the policeman called Don. 'This is her sister here,' he nodded towards Rashida. 'My guess is that the kid's wandered off to have a look at the rides so we should soon find her.'

The second policeman nodded understandingly at him. Charlie knew that's what they were both hoping. But they all knew that there was a possibility Sita wouldn't be found. She reached out and took Rashida's hand comfortingly. 'Let's pray and ask Jesus to help us find her,' she said.

'OK.' Rashida blinked back the tears and joined Charlie in prayer. 'Please Jesus, keep Sita safe and help us find her. Amen.'

It was only a short prayer, but all they had time for right now. Later on she would pray and ask Jesus to forgive her for encouraging Rashida to leave Sita on her own, Charlie promised herself.

Turn to page 66.

She couldn't keep the lion, no matter how much she wanted to. It wouldn't be fair. She had told Sita that they were going to try and win a prize for her, she couldn't let her down just because she liked the prize herself.

'Here you are, Sita,' Charlie forced herself to smile and she handed the little girl the precious lion.

'Thank you, Charlie,' Sita beamed with delight and clutched the lion happily. 'You are clever to win it!'

'Oh, Charlie, that's really kind of you!' Rashida smiled. 'Thank you!'

Alan shot her an admiring look. He often teased Charlie about her obsession for cuddly animals and here she was giving one away!

'I promised Sita that we'd try and win a prize for her,' Charlie explained ruefully. Alan gave her a thumbs up sign. A promise was a promise. But he knew how much it had cost Charlie to keep it.

They had such a good time at the fair that none of them wanted to go home. Sita was no trouble at all, she cuddled her lion and quite happily went on any ride they suggested. Charlie smiled as she watched her. It had been hard to give up the lion but she was glad she had done the right thing.

Turn to page 45.

'Don't be daft, we can't see the deer from the railway, they'd run away from any noise,' Charlie told him.

'Well, you probably won't see them anyway, they come out early in the morning or late at night, don't they?' Alan didn't like being called daft.

'Sometimes they come out in the day, so if we're quiet we might see them. Anyway, we'll be able to see the horses.'

Alan quite fancied seeing the animals himself so he agreed to visit the maze later.

Charlie carefully studied the map. 'We just go round the back of the house and down a narrow path,' she said. 'Come on.'

Map in hand, they walked around to the back of the big, rambling house. A narrow pathway ran alongside the house, leading down to what looked like a lane.

'This must be it,' Alan announced.

Charlie nodded. 'Now, remember, keep quiet or you'll scare the animals away.'

They walked down the pathway, then turned to the left, where it weaved through the wood. Every time a leaf rustled, the children looked over eagerly, hoping to see a glimpse of a deer among the tall growth of nettles and brambles, but no such luck. They did, however, see a grey squirrel scuttling up a tree, and Alan was sure he saw a rabbit peeping out of the bushes but when Charlie looked it had gone.

Turn to next page.

They came out of the wood to a clearing where several horses were grazing. Then suddenly, they heard a rustle behind them and turned around to see a deer springing out of the bushes. Charlie's face lit up and they both stood as still as statues, as the deer sprinted across the clearing and through the bushes on the other side.

'A deer!' Charlie clapped her hands, her eyes shining. 'We actually saw a deer!' Then her face fell. 'Oh no, we forgot to take a photo of it!'

'Maybe we'll see another one,' Alan took his camera out of his pocket. 'Still, at least we can get some shots of the horses.'

They both took several photos of the horses then decided to head for the railway.

Charlie consulted the map. 'We've got to go back through the wood a bit and go down a path on the right.'

'I hope the train's already in, otherwise we'll have to wait ages,' Alan said as they headed back towards the wood.

They soon found a path and set off down it. It was quite narrow and long. When they came to the end of it they were surprised to find themselves in what looked like a courtyard at the back of the Hall. A white van was parked in the yard, and two men were loading it up with furniture.

'Hey, I don't think we should be here, look!' Charlie pointed to a sign on the wall saying 'Private, Keep Out.' 'We must have come down the wrong path.'

Turn to next page.

'What do you mean *we*? You were the one who decided which way we had to go,' Alan retorted.

Charlie was too busy staring at the table the men were putting in the van to argue with him. There was a lot of carving on the legs and it looked really old. It must be an antique from the Hall. So was the other stuff by the look of it. Dad had told her some of the things at Birbeck Hall were worth thousands and thousands of pounds. What were the men doing with it?

She pulled Alan back into the shade of the trees so that men wouldn't spot them. 'What d'you reckon's going on?' she whispered. 'Why are they putting all that furniture in the van?'

'How do I know?' Alan shrugged. 'Maybe Lord Duncan's having a clear out.' He was too busy studying the map to try and figure out why they hadn't arrived at the railway as planned.

'Get real! Some of that stuff's really valuable! I reckon they're stealing it!'

If you think the men are stealing the stuff, turn to page 29.
If you think there is a simple explanation, turn to page 53.

Charlie didn't want to misjudge anyone but she was sure the vase had been stolen and she had to do something about it.

'OK, then let's just tell the guide that we think the vase is missing,' she suggested. 'We won't say anything about the women until she says it has been stolen. Then we can mention them. If the women are thieves, Alan, we've got to stop them before they steal anything else.'

Alan couldn't see anything wrong with that, so they raced along the corridor to a bedroom where the guide was telling the rest of the visitors all about the time Winston Churchill had come to stay for the weekend and how this was the room he slept in. She paused as Charlie and Alan ran in breathlessly.

'Please don't run around,' she told them firmly. 'There are many valuable things in the rooms, you could trip and knock something over.'

'Sorry! But we had to hurry and tell you!' Charlie gasped. She paused and chose her words carefully. 'We think that one of the vases is missing!'

'Really? Which vase?' the guide asked.

'The Chinese one downstairs in the hall.'

'That's impossible, the vase was there when I went past earlier and the alarm would have sounded if someone moved it,' the guide told her. 'Everything is alarmed, to make sure no one can take anything or go anywhere they shouldn't.'

Turn to next page.

'But it has gone! Take a look yourself if you don't believe me!'

Charlie's tone was so convincing that the guide ran to the top of the stairs and peered down to check for the vase.

'You're right! The vase has been stolen!' She exclaimed. 'But why didn't the alarms go off?' She reached out and picked up a lamp. Nothing happened. Frowning, she picked up a picture in a silver frame. Still nothing happened. 'The alarms have been turned off!' she gasped, turning to Charlie. 'Did you see anyone looking at the vase?' she demanded urgently. 'You must tell me if you saw anything suspicious at all, no matter how minor it seems!'

Quickly Charlie told her about the two women. The guide listened intently then ran down the stairs, two at a time, to the reception desk.

Turn to page 82.

'No we didn't, sorry.' Alan was right behind them. He and Charlie had arranged to write up their notes that evening and he was just on his way round when he saw Boffy and Jimbo walking up the path so he had quickened his pace. 'Somebody probably thought it was rubbish and put it in the bin,' he added.

Charlie bit her lip at the look of disappointment on Boffy and Jimbo's face. If Alan hadn't come along when he did she was sure she'd have owned up.

'I guess we'll just have to try and write it up again,' sighed Boffy. 'But some of those pictures were irreplaceable. I got them from mum's album.'

They both turned and walked dejectedly down the path.

'It's their own fault, they shouldn't have been so careless,' Alan felt just as guilty as Charlie. They both knew it was wrong to cheat, so they were trying to justify it. 'Anyway, I'm sick of them boasting, it'll take them down a peg or two if we beat them at the project!'

He was right, Charlie admitted, Boffy and Jimbo were always boasting about how clever they were. If they won this project they'd be insufferable.

Turn to page 64.

'That was brill!' exclaimed Charlie as they all got off the ride. 'I can't believe how high we went! I was scared to look down!'

'Me too!' laughed Rashida. 'We'd better go and buy Sita an ice-cream now, or she'll be moaning!' She looked over at the ticket office where she had left Sita but to her dismay there was no sign of her. 'Charlie!' she cried, grabbing her friend's arm in panic. 'Sita's gone!'

They all ran over to the kiosk, calling Sita's name, but there was no sign of her.

Rashida was distraught. 'I should never have left her on her own!' she cried. 'I should have stayed with her! Now she's lost and it's all my fault!'

'Stop panicking!' Alan told her firmly. 'She can't be far. She probably wandered off to look at something!'

'Don't worry, we'll split up and search for her!' Charlie reassured her friend. 'We'll soon find her, you'll see.'

'But what if we don't find her!' sobbed Rashida. 'What if someone's kidnapped her!'

Charlie felt her blood run cold. She'd read of things like that happening. They all should have known better than to leave Sita on her own. And she and Alan were just as much to blame as Rashida. But it was no good thinking about that now, they had to find the little girl and fast! Then she remembered that she'd seen a policeman patrolling by the gates of the park. He might still be there. 'Let's go and tell the policeman we saw by the gates that Sita is missing,' she suggested. 'He'll help us find her.'

If you think they should all split up and search for Sita, turn to page 62.
If you think they should find the policeman and tell him, turn to page 71.

Charlie spent a great evening with Rashida. She had lots of news of her cousins, Gemma and Justin. Gemma had written Charlie a long letter and there were photos to look at too. The evening passed so quickly, that Charlie could hardly believe it when Rashida's mum shouted upstairs that it was nine-thirty and Charlie's father had come to walk her home.

'I'll see you on Saturday then,' Charlie told Rashida. 'Now, don't forget, Nan wants you all to come to tea.'

'I won't forget,' her friend smiled. 'Oh, but I almost forgot something, we've been talking so much.' She opened her suitcase and handed Charlie a paper bag.

'Gemma, Justin, Stavros, Leroy and I all put together to buy you this. A sort of "hello" present. We thought you'd like it.'

Charlie was delighted. She loved getting presents. 'Thanks! That's really nice of you all,' she opended the bag and squealed in delight. It was a beautiful cuddly koala with a baby koala in its pouch.

'It's lovely!' she gasped. 'Really brilliant!'

Rashida smiled. 'Well, we know how you love cuddly animals.'

Charlie grinned back at her. Rashida knew how much she had wanted to keep the lion instead of giving it to Sita. Thank goodness she had made the right decision. The koalas were much better.

Turn to page 84.

Then everything happened at once. Some security guards came running through the entrance. Two of the guards stopped at the doors while the others talked to the guide. Then they came over to Charlie to ask for a description of the women. Then they all split up to search the Hall while the guide made an announcement asking everyone to come into the entrance hall.

The police soon arrived and an extensive search of the Hall and grounds began.

To everyone's astonishment, Lord Duncan was found bound and gagged in his private apartment, his safe had been burgled and two masked men had been caught trying to escape out of the window.

Not long afterwards, two women were also caught trying to sneak out of a side entrance and Charlie had no trouble identifying one of them as the woman who had stolen the vase.

Turn to the next page.

'And to think we thought it was going to be a boring day!' Alan said as he and Charlie cycled home.

'Yeah, wait until our folks know we helped catch some thieves!' grinned Charlie. 'Mind you, we haven't got much information for our project! I think we'll have to go to the library and read up some more about stately homes instead.'

Later that evening, Charlie and Alan both had a special guest – Lord Duncan himself. He had called to thank the children personally for helping catch the thieves. He gave them each a £20 gift voucher, and a complimentary ticket to visit Birbeck Hall any time they wished, as a reward. Both children were delighted. What an exciting day it had turned out to be!

The End

She had lots to tell her father as he walked her home that evening. She was chattering away happily for ages before she noticed how quiet Dad was. Oh dear, I hope he's not angry because I went to the fair with Rashida instead of going to Birbeck Hall, she thought. 'You don't mind that we didn't go to Birbeck Hall, do you, Dad?' she asked anxiously. 'Only you know how long it's been since I saw Rashida and it was great to spend the day together. But we will go tomorrow. Honest!'

Dad's answer really surprised her. 'To tell you the truth, Charlie, I'm pleased you didn't go,' he said. 'You see, I've just heard on the news that there was a burglary at Birbeck Hall today.'

The End

If you want to see what happens if they go to Birbeck Hall, turn to page 8 and make another choice.

They seemed to be travelling for hours. At first Charlie and Alan tried to stay alert and listen for sounds that might help them know where they were going. But after a while they found themselves drifting off to sleep.

The screech of brakes as the van jolted to a halt jarred them awake. They'd stopped! And it felt as if it had been a very sudden stop. They looked at each other, their frightened eyes shining in the darkness, their hearts pounding as a dozen frightening questions flooded their minds. What was happening? Why had they stopped so suddenly? And what were the men going to do with them?

A shaft of light dazzled them as the van doors were pulled open.

Turn to page 33.

Later, they were both busy writing up the project when a newsflash came on the TV saying that there had been a robbery at Birbeck Hall that afternoon. Charlie's dad immediately turned up the volume and they all listened intently as the news-reader described how Lord Duncan had been found tied up and gagged in his apartment, his safe robbed and several pieces of furniture and valuable paintings stolen. The newsreader went on to say that two children had alerted the staff to the robbery when they handed in a valuable painting they had found on the road.

'That's the one *I* found on the road!' Charlie cried as a picture of the horse painting flashed on the screen.

Charlie and Alan were really pleased that they had found the painting and returned it to Lord Duncan. At least that was one thing the thieves hadn't got away with.

But they felt really bad about Boffy and Jimbo's project. They should have returned that, just like they returned the painting. After all, Boffy and Jimbo had worked really hard and the project was valuable to them. They both knew how *they* would feel if they lost their project. In fact, they felt so guilty about it that they couldn't bring themselves to finish their own project. It just wouldn't be fair.

The End

Charlie thought for a moment. The booklet really would make a difference to their project. But she knew stealing it was wrong.

Alan took her silence as agreement and quickly slipped the booklet into his pocket. He glanced over at the lady on the till who was still busy serving.

Charlie bit her lip and looked around nervously. 'I don't think you should do that, Alan,' she whispered. 'Put it back.'

'Stop looking so worried, it's only a cheap booklet, no one will miss it,' Alan shrugged. He took a couple of postcards off the rack. 'We'd better pay for these though, the woman saw us come back in and might get suspicious if we walk out without buying anything.'

Charlie followed him as he walked over to the till. She felt really uncomfortable about the booklet he'd sneaked in his pocket. She tried to tell herself it was nothing to do with her, she hadn't stolen it. But she still felt guilty.

If you think Charlie should insist that Alan puts the booklet back, turn to page 91.
If you think Charlie should say nothing, turn to page 34.

Rashida shook her head. No matter how much she wanted to go on the Big Wheel she knew she couldn't leave Sita by herself. 'I'd better not leave Sita on her own, she might wander off and she doesn't know her way around here,' Rashida said reluctantly. 'You two go on the ride. I don't mind.'

'OK! See you later!'

Rashida watched enviously as Charlie and Alan ran to join the queue for the Big Wheel. She would have loved to have gone on with them but she was glad she had done the right thing and stayed with Sita. She would never forgive herself if she had wandered off and got lost. And neither would Mum and Dad!

'This is ace!' Alan shrieked. 'Look how high up we are!'

The Big Wheel was turning, carrying them higher and higher. Charlie squealed and clutched the sides of her seat tightly, even though she was firmly strapped in. The ground looked so far below. She could just make out Rashida and Sita standing by the ticket office watching them. Suddenly she felt really bad. She bet they would have liked to go on the ride too. It was really selfish of her and Alan to have left Rashida and Sita watching. Especially after Rashida's uncle had given them the money to go to the fair. They should have chosen a ride which they could all go on.

Turn to next page.

As soon as the ride finished, Charlie ran over to Rashida. 'I'll take Sita onto one of the smaller rides while you go on the Big Wheel, if you like,' she offered. 'Then we can find some rides we can all go on together.'

'Thanks!' Rashida's face broke into a big grin. 'But I don't want to go on by myself . . . '

'I'll come on with you,' Alan said eagerly. 'I'd love another go!'

Charlie turned to Sita. 'How about me and you going on the Carousel?' she suggested. 'I love going on those horses!'

'Yeah! Can I go on one that goes really fast?' Sita was already dashing off eagerly towards the Carousel.

'Hey, wait for me!' Charlie laughed.

Turn to next page.

Alan and Rashida joined them after their ride on the Big Wheel, and they all had another ride on the Carousel. Then Sita made a dash for the helter-skelter. 'Let's go on this!' she shouted.

'OK,' Rashida laughed. 'You coming?' she asked Alan and Charlie.

'You bet, I like the helter-skelter!' grinned Alan. 'Bet I'm the first one to the top!' He grabbed a mat, paid for his ticket and headed up the steps. Charlie close on his heels.

'Wait for us!' Rashida called as she and Sita chased after them.

After the helter-skelter, they all went on the dodgems. They steered the cars along the floor, laughing and squealing whenever they bumped into each other.

'This is brill! Much better than going to Birbeck Hall!' Charlie grinned when the dodgem ride finally ended. 'I'm glad we popped into your uncle's shop before we went out, Rashida, or we'd have missed you!'

'So am I!' Rashida told her. 'I think I'm going to enjoy my stay in England!'

The End

She couldn't keep quiet. If she said nothing she was just as much of a thief as Alan was. And she'd be letting everyone down; Dad, Nan, and most important of all, Jesus. Charlie grabbed Alan's arm and pulled him back. A woman looked curiously over at them. 'Hang on a minute, I want to swop those postcards for a different one,' she said quickly.

'But these were the best!' protested Alan.

'No they weren't.' Charlie dragged him back to the postcard rack.

As soon as they reached it she hissed. 'I'm not going out of this shop until you put that booklet back!'

'What?' Alan looked at her as if she'd gone mad. 'But we need it for the project.'

'Not that bad, we don't!' Charlie felt more confident now. 'It's wrong to steal! You've got to put it back!'

'OK.' Alan knew she was right. He glanced around to make sure no one was looking, then put the booklet back on the rack.

'Good, now let's get out of here,' Charlie said. They could buy some postcards later. Right now she just wanted to get as far away from the shop as possible. She couldn't believe that Alan had been prepared to steal something and she had almost let him.

As they went to leave the shop the woman who had been looking curiously at them walked over.

Turn to next page.

'I'm glad you put that booklet back, young man,' she said. 'I'd hate to have arrested you both for shoplifting!'

Charlie and Alan stared at each other in a mixture of relief and horror. The woman had been watching them!

Thank goodness Charlie had spoken up and made Alan put the booklet back or they would both have been in big trouble!

'Phew! That was a close shave! Thanks, Charlie,' Alan said when they were both safely outside. 'I dunno what made me steal that booklet, it was a dumb thing to do. But I tell you something, I'll never steal anything again. Never.'

Charlie smiled. She was pleased about that. And she knew Jesus would be too.

The End

Most of the prizes were furry toys, mainly different kinds of teddies, although there were a couple of watches and some goldfish that were transferred into plastic bags of water for you to take home. Charlie didn't want to win a goldfish, she hated the thought of any animal kept in a closed space like a cage or bowl. It seemed cruel. She didn't think much of teddies either.

'What shall we try and win?' she asked Sita.

The little girl carefully studied the array of furry toys in front of her. 'The lion!' she decided, pointing to a cute furry lion that Charlie hadn't noticed, partly hidden behind a blue teddy bear. It had a card around its neck marked number twenty. 'I want the lion!'

Charlie wanted the lion too. It was beautiful. She adored cuddly animals and already had several at home including a kangaroo from her trip to Australia. 'Me too!' she said. 'It's really sweet, isn't it?'

It cost fifty pence for three hoops, so Charlie handed over a pound for six hoops and gave three to Sita. 'You go first,' she said.

Sita threw her hoops very carefully but they all missed their target.

'Oh no, I missed!' she wailed. 'You try, Charlie. You can do it!'

Charlie's second hoop hovered over peg number 5 then toppled off. 'Sorry,' she apologised, seeing the crestfallen look on Sita's face when the last hoop had been thrown.

Turn to next page.

'Can we have another go? Please!' begged Sita. 'Just one more!'

'What are you trying to win?' asked Rashida as she and Alan joined them.

'That lion, isn't it lovely!' Sita pointed eagerly to it.

Charlie paid for six more rings and handed three to Sita. The little girl carefully took aim and threw them, one by one, over the pegs. 'Missed again!' she said disappointedly.

'Never mind, have a lollipop!' The man in charge of the stall handed her a toffee lollipop as a consolation prize. He kept a jar of them for all the disappointed little kids. Sita took the lollipop gratefully but her heart was still set on the lion.

'Go for it Charlie!' Alan shouted as Charlie threw her hoops. To her amazement the last hoop landed over number twenty. She'd done it! She'd won the lion!

'Hey, great shot!' Alan whacked her across the back as the man handed her the precious lion.

'Thanks!' Charlie held the lion proudly. Another one for her collection. Then she noticed Sita looking at her, expectantly. Oh no, she expected Charlie to give her the lion. But she hadn't promised to do that, had she? She hadn't meant Sita could keep *her* prize. What was she going to do?

If you think Charlie should give the lion to Sita, turn to page 73.
If you think Charlie should keep the lion herself, turn to page 10.

The man tied up in the chair, who was evidently Lord Duncan, turned his head to look over at Charlie and Alan, trying to tell them with his eyes not to be afraid. They tried to relax. After all, a maid or someone was bound to come in soon to see Lord Duncan about something. It wouldn't be long before they were discovered and untied.

Suddenly, Charlie remembered that the guide had told them that both Lord and Lady Duncan were out for the day. Why Lord Duncan had still been there when the thieves arrived she had no idea, but it was evident that no one would come into his private quarters. Not until much later that evening anyway. It looked as if they were going to be tied up for a long time. She wished they had carried on with the rest of the group instead of sneaking into the private quarters! She had known it was wrong to trespass into other people's private property. If only she had spoken up about it, instead of following Alan. But it was too late to wish that now. All they could do was pray that Lady Duncan would come home early and discover them.

The End

If you want to know what would have happened if they'd looked around the grounds first, turn to page 13 and make another choice.

'Oh, come on! Sita will be okay for a few minutes,' Alan persuaded her.

Rashida really did want to go on the ride. And Alan was right, it was only for a few minutes. She bent down to speak to her younger sister. 'Listen Sita, I'm going on the Big Wheel with Charlie and Alan so you must wait here for me. OK? You mustn't go off anywhere else. You have to stay right here and wait until we come off. D'you understand?'

Sita didn't fancy that at all. She screwed up her face in disappointment. 'I want to go on the Big Wheel too!'

'You can't, you're too small,' Charlie explained. 'Tell you what, if you're a good girl and wait here for us we'll buy you an ice-cream when we come off.'

Sita's face brightened. 'Promise?' she asked her sister, not knowing Charlie well enough to rely on her keeping her word.

'Promise!' Rashida nodded.

'OK,' Sita agreed.

'Quick, everyone's getting off. It'll be starting in a minute!' Alan called.

With a quick wave to Sita, Rashida ran to join her friends in the queue.

Turn to page 80.